TILLY'S HOUSE

Written and illustrated by
FAITH JAQUES

A Margaret K. McElderry Book
Atheneum   1979   New York

For Polly Morgan

Library of Congress Cataloguing in Publication Data

Jaques, Faith.
 Tilly's House.

 "A Margaret K. McElderry book."
 SUMMARY: Tilly leaves the dollhouse where she works
as a kitchen maid to find a home of her own.
 [1. Dolls–Fiction] I. Title.
PZ8.9.J26Ti [E] 78–31105
ISBN 0–689–50138–2

Manufactured in Great Britain

First American Edition

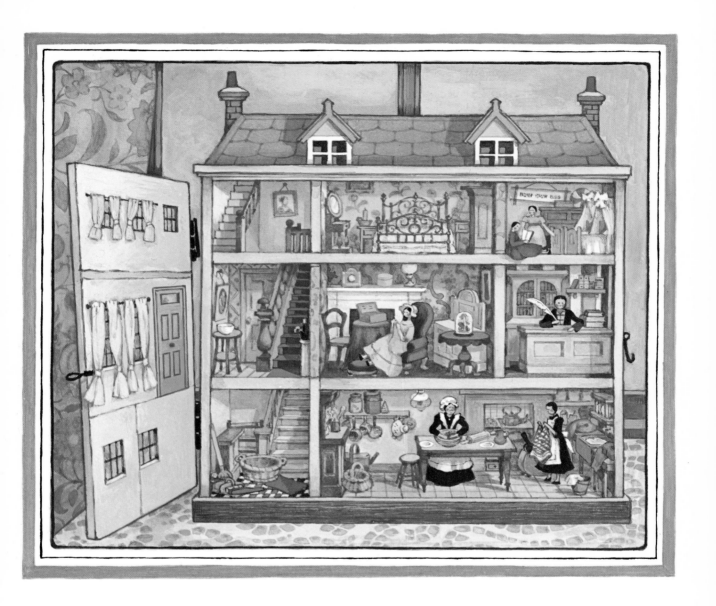

Upstairs in the dolls' house there lived a family of wooden dolls.
Father worked in his study all day, while Mother did her
mending in the parlor. The two children played in the nursery
on the floor above.

    Downstairs in the kitchen Cook prepared the meals, and gave
orders to Tilly, the kitchenmaid.

Poor Tilly! Every day she got up at five to clean out the grates and lay the fires. She cleared the breakfast table, made the beds, and swept and cleaned and scrubbed and polished all day long. After supper she did the washing-up and mopped the kitchen floor. And all the time Cook nagged at her, and shouted at her, and told her she must work still harder.

"I wouldn't mind how hard I worked if I had a home of my own," Tilly said to herself one night as she washed a pile of dirty dishes. "But I'm sick and tired of Cook ordering me around all day, with never a word of thanks."

Just then Cook cried out, "Tilly! Make sure you do the ironing before you go to bed!" When Tilly had finished she was worn out.

She climbed the stairs to her little room in the attic and sank onto the bed. "Nothing will ever change," she thought wearily. "I'll be washing and scrubbing all my life if I stay here. I've got to find a place where I can be free and decide things for myself." Suddenly she jumped off the bed. "I'll walk out!" she cried. "There's no time like the present – I'll leave straight away and find a home of my own!"

Tilly brought out her canvas bag, packed her knitting and her sewing box, picked up her big umbrella and put on her shawl. Then she blew out the candle, shut the door behind her, and tiptoed down the stairs and to the basement.

The front wall of the dolls' house hung on a broken hinge. Tilly edged outside and found herself standing on a lacy cloth which covered a wooden chest.

She was in a child's bedroom and the floor was a long way
below. "Come on, now, Tilly," she said to herself, "she who
hesitates is lost." She hooked her umbrella on the edge of the
chest and slid down it. Her legs waved wildly, but she got a
foothold in the lacy holes of the cloth and worked her way
down by lowering the umbrella and hooking it in the holes as
she went.

At last Tilly reached the hem and jumped to the ground. "I'm free!" she whispered, shaking with excitement. The moon shone brightly through the half-drawn curtains, making silver squares upon the floor as she crept past the sleeping child and across the room. There was no sound but the tiny tapping of her wooden feet.

The door was open just a crack, and Tilly slipped through.

The door opened onto a landing. Tilly peered anxiously down the stairs. "How deep they are!" she thought. "But I've got to get down them somehow. Oh well, nothing venture, nothing gain." She tucked the umbrella through the flap of the canvas bag, and managed to get to the bottom by hanging from the edge of every stair and dropping to the one below.

By the time she reached the hall Tilly was exhausted. She could go no further, so she decided to find somewhere for the night and look for a home the next day. She peeped into a cupboard under the stairs. There she saw a tall wicker basket with a red blanket in it.

"That will do nicely," thought Tilly, and she stepped inside.

She stretched out on the blanket and slept soundly until early morning, when a scratching sound woke her. Tilly sat up with a start. A round furry face was looking through the wire door of the basket. It belonged to a teddy bear.

"What are *you* doing here?" he asked. "Don't you know you're in the cat's traveling-basket? She'll be furious!" He sat down beside Tilly. "My name's Edward," he added more gently.

"Mine's Tilly," answered Tilly. "I was just having a nap. I'm looking for somewhere to live, but I've come a long way and I had to rest." Edward had such a kind face that she soon found herself telling him all about her life in the dolls' house. "So you see," she said firmly, "I *must* find a home of my own."

"I'll help you," said Edward. "Let's look around the house and see if we can find somewhere you fancy."

They left the cupboard and Edward led her along the hall. He showed her a coat which was lying over a chair.

"Why don't you settle down in one of the pockets?" he asked. "You'd be quite snug."

"Dear me, no!" replied Tilly rather sharply. "What do you think would become of me when the owner wanted to wear it? That won't do. What's that room over there?"

"That's the sitting-room," said Edward. They went inside and Tilly stared around her.

"Now, what about the bookcase?" Edward suggested. "Here's a cosy space on the bottom shelf. Couldn't you make a home in there, between the books?"

"I should think not!" said Tilly indignantly. "*I* don't want to get squashed when somebody puts a book in."

Edward was trying hard to be helpful. He led Tilly to an armchair and said, "Look, there's plenty of room under here. No one would see you behind the chair cover."

"Until they swept the carpet," Tilly said crisply. "I can see there isn't anywhere here that's any use. What about the other rooms – surely you can find somewhere better?"

"Let's try the kitchen," said Edward patiently. He led the way back across the hall. "Now, what about the kitchen cupboard? It's warm and safe, even though it's a bit dark."

"I'd never get a moment's peace!" sniffed Tilly. "People will be clattering the cups and saucers about all day long. Really, Edward, you're not very practical."

Edward looked crestfallen. "I'm sorry," said Tilly, "but I don't want a part of someone else's home. I want a home that's all my own. I don't mind how dirty or shabby it is – I'll clean it and make things for it, and work hard to make it nice. Can't you think of *anything*?"

"It's very difficult," said Edward, sighing heavily, "I don't know where else to look." Suddenly his face brightened.

"I know!" he cried. "The old greenhouse at the bottom of the garden! No one's been near it for years, and it's full of junk. I'm sure you could make a nice home there."

"Good," said Tilly at once, collecting her things. "How do I get there?"

"I'll take you," said Edward. He led her to the back door and held up the cat-flap so she could climb through.

Tilly was in the open air for the first time in her life. A jungle
of weeds and grasses and wild flowers arched over her and high
above was the great expanse of sky. Huge insects rustled in the
grass, and striped monsters buzzed overhead.

"I'll lead the way," said Edward, setting off at a steady pace.
Tilly clutched her umbrella and followed him as best she could.

It was hard going. Tilly toiled along through the undergrowth on her wobbly little legs. She had never walked so far before and soon felt weary, but she knew she must be brave and not give up.

"Really," she thought disapprovingly as she struggled on, "this garden is most untidy and badly kept. I'd never let it get in such a state if it were mine."

"This is it," said Edward at last. "Look, the bottom of the door's rotted, so we can get in underneath."

Once inside the greenhouse, Tilly looked around with interest. A bench ran along the walls, cluttered with cracked flower-pots, raffia and twine, sticks and twigs and other useful things. In the corner was a dripping water-tap, and near it, half-hidden by a litter of flower-pots, a dirty old box lay on its side.

"I think I'll have a look at that box," said Tilly. "Wait here, Edward. Now, how do I get up on the bench?"

She thought for a moment, then scrambled up the spout of a watering can and climbed to the rim. Using her trusty umbrella she hoisted herself up to the seat of a stool, and from there managed to haul herself onto the bench. She examined the box.

"I believe this will do!" she thought triumphantly.

"I've found it, Edward!" she cried, as she slithered down to the floor again. "That box is just right for a house! It's filthy, but I'll clean it up and then I'll start making furniture for it. I'll need all sorts of bits and pieces. Can you help?"

"Of course," said Edward. "What do you think you'll need?"

"Things to hold water," said Tilly, "and bits of cloth, and little boxes. Anything! Whatever you can find!"

"Leave it to me," said Edward, "I'll see what there is at home."

Tilly was so excited she hardly noticed him going. She cleared a space around her box and inspected some flower-pots nearby. She thought some of the wilted plants might put out shoots if she watered them. And the gaily colored packets lying on the bench might contain seeds.

"Why, I can even make a garden!" she said delightedly.

But first of all the house had to be cleaned from top to bottom.
Tilly rolled up her sleeves and set to work with a broom she had
made out of tiny twigs, attached with twine to a piece of stick.
She looked up to see a shiny black beetle shuffling towards her.
Tilly thrust the broom at it and it scuttled away. "Off with you!"
she cried. "I won't have strangers in my house. And don't you
dare come back!"

Edward soon returned. "Just see what I've got!" he said proudly, untying a huge bundle of oddments from the trashcan. Tilly had never seen plastic and foam rubber and drip-dry cotton, so she was amazed when Edward explained what everything was. He had picked her some flowers, too, and Tilly thanked him warmly.

"Now, Edward," she said firmly, "I've got a lot to do, so you must let me get on with it. Come back and see my house in a week."

After Edward left Tilly sorted through all the oddments. She
knew she could find a use for everything, but first she must do
some washing. She rolled an egg-cup near the water-tap and
climbed up to turn the water on. "Where there's a will there's a
way," thought Tilly, as she opened out a paper-clip to make a
handle for a plastic carton. She lowered the carton into the bucket
and hauled it up when it was full.

Soon Tilly had filled several containers. She put aside some bits of
soap, and ladled water into three plastic jars. Then she removed
the foam rubber from an oven glove, and cut up everything made
of cloth into small pieces. She washed these carefully and hung
them on sticks along the front of the box. They dried without
creasing. "How much easier life in the dolls' house would have been
without all that ironing," thought Tilly wistfully.

Tilly took down the washing and got out her sewing box. She patched a hole in a pot-holder and another in a piece she had cut from an apron.

"Fancy throwing all this away, just for the want of a bit of mending," she thought, as she snipped off a thread. "Everyone knows a stitch in time saves nine."

She cut two lengths from the rest of the apron, for sheets.

Then Tilly laid a long piece from the quilted cover of a hot-water bottle over three matchboxes. It would make a comfortable chair, she thought.

She folded the foot of a sock and used it to pad the seat. Then she cut a piece of foam rubber to fit on a plastic bottle-top.

"That will be a stool," she said to herself. "I'll make a frilly flounce for it later."

Next day Tilly lined an old
eyeglass case with the upper
part of the sock.

   She used a square of foam
rubber for a pillow, and made
a flowered pillow-case to
match the sheets. A piece of
quilt was just right for a
bedspread.

   Soon she had made a
snug little bed. It was much
nicer than the hard bed she
had slept on in the dolls'
house.

There was some crumpled
wrapping paper in Edward's
bundle. It had "Merry
Christmas" and sprigs of holly
all over it.

   "Waste not, want not,"
said Tilly to herself. "I'll use it
for wallpaper." She smoothed
it out, and pinned it round the
walls of the box, standing on a
ladder she had made from
sticks and twine. Then she sat
down and planned all the
things she still had to do.

How Tilly worked! She didn't stop for a minute. She put earth in the hollows of an egg-box and planted the daisy root that Edward had brought. Then she arranged the furniture, setting out a table with a cloth over it, and a flower-vase on a pillar, and a full-length mirror, slightly cracked.

Tilly stood back and surveyed her new home with delight.

"Later on I must make some curtains for the front, and tidy up
the bench," she thought, "but this will do beautifully for now."

She was ready and waiting when Edward climbed up to the bench.

"Why, Tilly!" cried Edward. "It's the prettiest little house I've
ever seen. How *clever* you are!"

Tilly's varnished face shone with pride.

Tilly offered Edward the best chair and they settled down for
a contented evening in the snug little house. When it grew dark
they sat in the soft candlelight and talked of Tilly's life as a
kitchenmaid, and her adventures since she left the dolls' house.

"It just shows what can be done," said Edward, "with a bit of
common sense and a good strong umbrella."

"And the help of a good kind friend!" added Tilly happily.